Space Dog

Visits Planet Earth

Vivian French
Illustrated by Sue Heap

Hodder
Children's
Books
a division of Hodder Headline

To Joe

CHAPTER ONE

It was late in the evening.

Big Sun
and Little
Sun were
tucked up
in bed.

Blue Moon
was sitting
on a cloud,
shining.

Purple Moon was trying to
bake a cake on a very grumpy
star. There was a strong smell
of burning.
"BOTHER!" said Purple Moon.

Green Moon blew her nose
loudly.

Space Dog waved from his kennel.

"Hi there, Green Moon!"
Green Moon sneezed a HUGE
sneeze, "AAAATTCHOOOO!!!"

Space Dog's
nightcap blew
away.

"Sorry," said Green Moon.
"It's the smoke.

Purple Moon's burnt three
cakes already, and the smell
gets up my nose."

She sneezed again, and a cloud
of smoke blew in through Space
Dog's open window just as—

BRRRRRRINGGGGG!

The bone phone
rang.
Space Dog banged
his window shut
and hurried to
answer it.

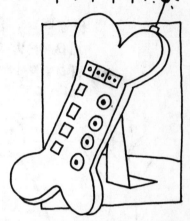

"Hello! Space Dog here! How
can I help you?"
There was a snuffling noise.
Then a voice sang:

"Happy Birthday to me
Happy Birthday to me
Happy Birthday Pink Arkle,
Happy Birthday to me!"

Space Dog frowned. "Pink Arkle!" he said. "This phone is for EMERGENCIES only! Are you having an emergency?"

"A what?" asked Pink Arkle. Space Dog sighed. "Are you all right?" he asked.

Space Dog never heard Pink Arkle's answer.

Someone sneezed the most enormous sneeze. Space Dog's kennel shook and the bone phone went dead.

Space Dog ran to the window
to look out.

Purple Moon
and Blue Moon's
mouths were
wide open.

Big Sun was peering over the
edge of his cloud.
Little Sun was peeping over
Big Sun's shoulder.

Green Moon was nowhere
to be seen.

"WOOF! Green Moon has sneezed herself away!" said Space Dog.

"I'd better find her!"

"Quick!" called
Blue Moon. "She
went THAT way!
Towards the
Grisly Asteroids!"

"Hurry!" shouted Purple Moon.

"She was
going
REALLY fast!"

13

"I'll find her!" said Space Dog. And up . . . and away . . . he flew.

Blue Moon and Purple Moon
nodded to each other as Space
Dog disappeared.
"She'll soon be home," they
said. "Space Dog will find her."

Space Dog flew as fast as he could. There was no sign of Green Moon.

"Oh, dear," he said. "This part of the galaxy is NOT safe—

WHOOPS!" Space Dog did a
quick loop around a large Grisly
Asteroid . . . and hurried on.

"Woof. No sign of Green Moon there. Wherever can she— WOOOOOOOOOFFFFFFFF!!!"

Space Dog screeched to a stop. In front of him was a GIGANTIC web.

It was hanging
from a whole
family of Grisly
Asteroids, and
it stretched
down . . .
and down . . .
into Lower
Space.

In the middle
of the web
were two
Flugs . . .
an Urk . . .

a large Pink Arkle . . .

and Green Moon.

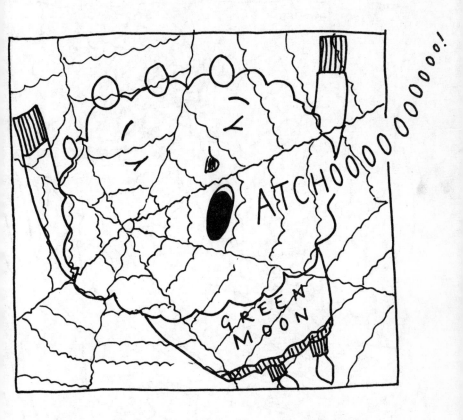

CHAPTER TWO

Green Moon sneezed noisily as Space Dog flew nearer.

"Space Dog!" she said. "I'm stuck! ATCHOOO!"

The web shook and trembled.

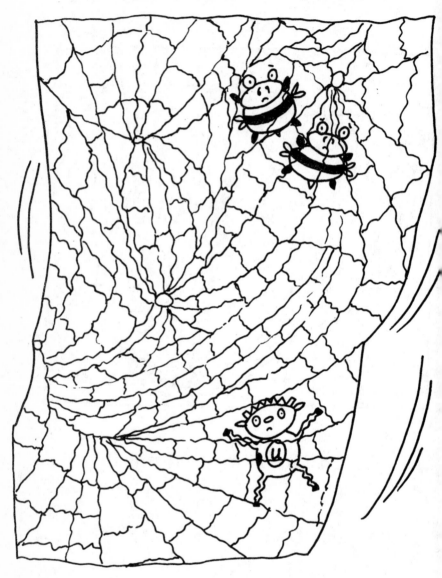

The Flugs and the Urk went pale.

"Hello, Space Dog," said Pink
Arkle cheerfully. "I knew
you'd come."

"Urk," said the Urk.

"Can you pull me out?" Green
Moon asked anxiously.
"Grab my paw," said Space Dog.

Green Moon held on tightly.
Space Dog flipped his tail .
"One . . . two . . . three . . .
GO!" he barked, and roared
away from the web.

The web stretched . . .
    and stretched . . .
        and stretched . . .
"I'm still stuck!" gasped Green
Moon. "And my arms are
getting longer—"
TWANGGGGGGGG!!!

Green Moon came unstuck.
She and Space Dog spun
head over heels.

The Urk and the two Flugs were
hurled into space as the web
twanged back again.

"WHEEEEEE!!!" shouted Pink Arkle.

"THANK YOU, Space Dog," said Green Moon as they stopped spinning. "ATCHOO! Can we go home now?"

"Yes," said Space Dog. "But first I need to check this out. Webs stretched across space are DANGEROUS."

"Coooeee!" It was Pink Arkle.
"Look at me!"
Space Dog did a back flip.

6

"Pink Arkle," he said as he
hovered a little closer, "you're
not stuck!"

"Oh no." Pink Arkle bounced happily. "The web only sticks to Urks and Flugs and Green Moons."

Very carefully Space Dog put out his paw and touched the edge of the web. The grey gooey threads clung tightly to his fur.

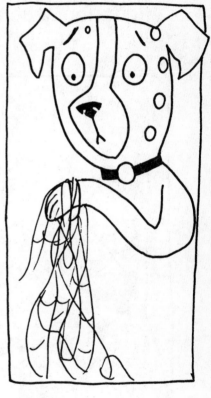

"YUCK!" Space Dog shook himself until his paw was free. "Why don't YOU stick, Pink Arkle?"

"BOING!" shrugged Pink Arkle.
Space Dog thought for a
moment. "Hmm," he said. "Do
you fancy an adventure?"

Pink Arkle looked hopeful.
"Will there be cake? and buns?"

"I don't know," said Space Dog. He pointed at the sticky web. "But I've got a feeling that this goes all the way to Planet Earth."

"EARTH!" gasped Green Moon. "you can't go there! It's full of horrid aliens with ten toes and hairy heads!"

"I know," said Space Dog. "But I must get rid of the web!"

CHAPTER THREE

Space Dog left Pink Arkle and
Green Moon together while he
zoomed back to his kennel. He
grabbed an earth cap . . . and
dashed out again.

"Green Moon's quite safe!"
he called as he whizzed over
Blue Moon's head. "She'll be
back soon!"

Green Moon was looking worried
when Space Dog came back.
"Space Dog," she whispered,
"are you QUITE sure about
Pink Arkle? He says he was
once a PIRATE!"

"Don't worry," Space Dog said.
"He wasn't a very scary
pirate . . . " He turned to
Pink Arkle. "Are you ready?

You can hang on to my tail."
Pink Arkle shook his head
"No," he said. "I'm going to
slide down to the cake and the
buns. Yum yum."

Space Dog gave
Pink Arkle a
paws-up sign.
He began the
countdown. "Five . . . four . . .
three . . . two . . . ONE!!"
And Space Dog
zoomed away.

Pink Arkle slid
happily down
the web beside
him.
Down and down
they went.
Past planets.
Past stars.
And the web
still went on . . .

Down and down they went,
until Pink Arkle began to cough.

"Sorry, Pink Arkle," said Space
Dog. "That's Planet Earth
for you. Lots of smoke and
bad smells."
"Nasty," said Pink Arkle, and he
stopped sliding. "I don't like it!"

Slowly and carefully, Space Dog
flew nearer and nearer to Planet
Earth. The web stretched down
through the patchy grey clouds.
Here and there Space Dog could
see treetops and pointed roofs.
And something else . . .

"THAT'S IT!" said Space Dog and
clapped his paws. "THAT's where
the web comes from!

I'm going to land," he told Pink
Arkle. "If anything happens to
me – run!"

He looked at the Pink Arkle's
puzzled face. "I mean, climb!
Climb back up the web as fast
as you can go!"

On nearly every pointed roof
was a round tube with a hole
in the end.
A long grey sticky thread
oozed out of every tube.
Above the tubes the threads
twisted into ropes. The ropes
stretched up into the sky . . .
and held the web firmly tied
to Planet Earth.

Space Dog thought hard.
"I can't see any Earth Aliens. I
need to get closer still."

Space Dog dived through a dark grey cloud. "WOOOWWLLL!" he howled. He was in the middle of a rainstorm.

Landing on a roof he skidded
down behind a roof tube for
shelter . . . and came face-to-face
with something nasty.
Something very nasty indeed.
It had seven legs, five eyes, and
VERY sharp teeth . . .

"KING
SPINDLER!"
yelled Space
Dog.

But in a flash, King Spindler had thrown out a long line – and Space Dog was tied up like a parcel.

"RUN!! PINK ARKLE – RUN!!" Space Dog shouted up to the sky.

"TEE HEE!" cackled King Spindler.
"Now all space belongs to ME!"

No more Space Dog –
TEE HEE HEE!"

CHAPTER FOUR

Up above Planet Earth, Pink Arkle was sitting and singing to himself.

" It's a great mistake
if there isn't any cake!
But life can be fun
with a bun!"

He was so pleased with his song
that he started to sing it again,
but— "WHAT'S THAT?"
Pink Arkle sat bolt upright.
"I hear Space Dog! OOH! OOH!
Space Dog is calling Pink Arkle!
SPACE DOG SAYS . . .

And Pink Arkle began slipping
and sliding down the web as
fast as he could go.
Down on Planet Earth Space
Dog was tied so tightly that
he couldn't move.

Worst of all, Spindlers were
creeping out from every rooftop.
They gazed at him with boggling
beady eyes.

One by one they swung nearer
and nearer, snapping their very
sharp teeth as they came.

"TEE HEE!" said King Spindler.
"GOOD NEWS, my leggy
friends! SPACE IS OURS!"
"YEAH! YEAH! YEAH!" The
Spindlers raised their legs and
cheered loudly.

"But first – WHAT SHALL WE
DO WITH SPACE DOG?"

CRASHHHHHHHHHHHHHH!!!
Pink Arkle hadn't meant to fall
– SPLATTTTTT!!
on top of King Spindler.

But, as Space Dog said afterwards, it couldn't have been better.

"Nooooooo!" wailed the Spindlers. "It's raining Pink Arkles!" And they threw themselves down on their faces.

Pink Arkle stayed sitting where
he had landed.
"Where's the bun?" he asked.

It did not take long for Pink
Arkle to untie Space Dog.
"Well done!" said Space Dog.
"Pink Arkle, you're a hero!

Now – I've got an idea!"
Space Dog folded his arms and
glared at the Spindlers.
"YOU made this horrible web –
so YOU can roll it up! All the
way to the Grisly Asteroids! And
if you DON'T hurry, it'll rain
Pink Arkles all over again!"

Pink Arkle waved his trunk.
"BOING! BOING!" he agreed.

By the time they
reached the
Grisly Asteroids
the Spindlers
were puffing and
panting.

So was Space
Dog. He had
flown all the
way from
Planet Earth
with Pink Arkle
hanging on to
his tail.

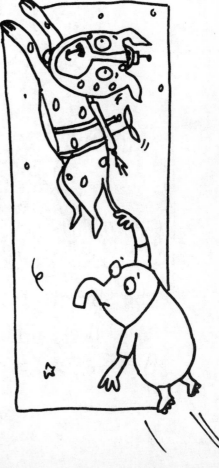

"Hello Green Moon!" said Space Dog as they landed on the biggest asteroid. "We're just going to roll this web into a crater forever and ever. AREN'T we, Spindlers?"

The Spindlers waved their legs. "And there'll be NO MORE WEBS – will there?"

"Just as you say, Mr Space Dog,"
whispered the Spindlers.
"Fine," said Space Dog.
"Green Moon, Pink Arkle – let's
be getting back."
Pink Arkle didn't answer. He
was sniffing the air with a
beautiful smile on his face.
"CAKE!" he said "CAKE!"

Space Dog sniffed too.
"So it is!" he said. "Purple Moon
must have got it right at last!
We'd better hurry home!"
And Green Moon, Pink Arkle
and Space Dog flew
up . . .

   and off . . .

     and away . . .